MAGIC MYSTERY

ECRET OF THE MARSH

MAOKS

First published in 1985 by Macmillan Children's Books a division of Macmillan Publishers Ltd. London and Basingstoke
© 1985 The Mushroom Writers' and Artists' Workshop Ltd.   ISBN 0 333 38887 9 HB   ISBN 0 333 38888 7 PB
Magic Mystery Books are produced by Mushroom Books Ltd. 9 Newburgh Street London W1V 1LH
Origination by Newsele S.R.L. (UK) 01·734 0628 Printed in Italy in association with Keats European Ltd.

MAGIC MYSTERY CLUB

Calling the hawk-eyed, cunning and sharp-witted. Join the Magic Mystery Club! You will receive a Special Investigator's pack containing: a Magic Mystery Club badge, personalised I.D. card, code maker/breaker kit and a top secret document.

All you have to do is write your age and your name and address in BLOCK CAPITALS on a piece of paper and send it, with a postal order for 50p to:

YM3431
9 Newburgh Street, London W1V 1LH.

Open to residents of the UK and Republic of Ireland only.

Find the clues, solve the mystery and and make a different story every time.

When you read, "Wait until the coast is clear and get closer to the factory on page 41. Or sneak through the grass and go on to Jill's on page 38.", *you* have to decide what to do, then turn to the page you have chosen. It might be ahead, or it might be behind.

Use your skill to make the right choice. If you are hawk-eyed, cunning and sharp-witted, you'll spot the clues, outwit the enemies and uncover the secret. But the *Magic Mystery* doesn't end there. Each story has more than one ending. Some routes lead to success: on some pages you'll catch the villain. Other routes lead to failure: on some pages the villain will catch you! Whatever happens, remember – find the clues, solve the mystery – and make a different story every time.

Solve the mystery of
THE MARSH

The marsh is a lonely place, crossed by only one road which leads to a derelict farm built on the only really dry land for miles.

Your grandfather taught you how to cross the marsh safely by identifying the grasses which grow on firm ground.

You have learned a lot about nature from watching the rare plants and birds on the marsh. You often go there to be alone. But at this moment your marsh is one of the most dangerous places in the world.

Find out why. Go to page 1.

One morning of the holiday, you set off to visit your science teacher. A strange idea? Well, she's also your cousin, Jill.

A van passes you on its way to the old farm, which has recently been converted to a small factory. A rather unusual load for a greengrocer to deliver, you think.

You haven't been up here since the factory opened, but you know that Jill is worried about the pollution it is causing.

If you want to follow the van, go to page 22.
Or, if you want to go on to Jill's, go to page 38.

2

This is your first close look at the factory.

You memorise as much as you can.

A gate in the fence opens and two security guards come out. You crouch low in the grass as they walk in your direction.

If you want to wait until the coast is clear and get closer to the factory, go to page 41. ☞

Or sneak through the grass and go on to Jill's. Go to page 38. ☞

"The factory poses a serious threat to the countryside," says Jill.

"What do you mean?" questions someone.

"The pollution," Jill begins.

"A little dirt never hurt anyone," scoffs the man.

"The factory's never bothered us," says a woman.

"What about the traffic?" suggests Jill.

"More trade for my garage," laughs a local trader.

The meeting is a failure. No one wants to know how bad things are. What can you do? Two ideas occur to you.

You could go to the local police and tell them the whole story. Go to page 40. ☞

Or you could go down to the old church, where Jill's friends are camping, and ask them to help you search for proof that the factory is harmful. Go to page 16. ☞

The file is all about you!

Your name, address, photograph, details of your family!

"We know all about you," says the director behind you. "Your grandfather, who knew the marsh so well. Your cousin, so interested in pollution."

He tells you that his security men have files on many local people. Also, all the time you have been in the factory, you have been watched on closed-circuit television.

"Now, please leave. Do not come back without an invitation."

You are driven down to the main road.

If you want time to think, cross the marsh to the village. Go to page 28.
Or hurry along the main road to page 13.

"Excuse me," says the sergeant. "Have you just come from the factory?"
You tell him that you've just left.
"They rang the station to report the theft of a box of perfumes – rather like the one you have there."

"I haven't stolen anything," you protest. "It's a frame!"
Rather to your surprise, the sergeant just nods. "Can you help us?" he asks. "You're free to say 'no', but, if you could come down to the station soon, we'd be most grateful."

Is this an arrest? He did say you needn't go!

If you want to go to the police station, go to page 40.

Or, if you want to go home now, promise to call later and go to page 13.

"Look at this," says Jill, handing Tony a starling's nest with three cold eggs. "My cousin here found this near the factory." She shows him some stiff brown grass, saying, "This comes from behind the factory. Just look at it. And see this withered fern. It's covered with some sort of gummy stuff. It can barely photosynthesize food."

"You've given me samples of pollution before," says Tony. "But they don't prove anything. Hang on though, this fern has a familiar smell. It's like paint. Wasn't there a story in yesterday's daily paper about pollution being discovered by the smell of paint?"

"I didn't keep the paper," Jill tells him. "But it'll be in the library."

If you want to look up the article, go to the library on page 39.
Or, if you want to attend Jill's meeting, go to page 46.

The director is in his office, but he doesn't see you.

You are surprised to see a refrigerator. Perhaps he keeps samples in it.

If you want to talk to the director, wait until he turns around, and go to page 36.

Or, if you want to investigate the basement, go out into the corridor and close the door. Go to page 31.

So far, so good.

The containers are heavy and so probably full. They are firmly sealed, but don't feel cold. Perhaps they're vacuum flasks.

The fume cupboards have extractor fans to the outside. You notice there is no smell .   All the fumes are going outside!

You notice the stairs to the basement, and the door to the office.

Go down to the basement on page 31.
Or to the office on page 7.

The guard takes an instant photograph of you and makes you write your name and address on the back.

"I shan't bother the director about this, or I'll be getting the sack. I'll let you go this time, if you agree not to come back. All right?"

Do you trust him? Is he really letting you off lightly?

If you want to insist on seeing the director, go to page 36.
Or follow the guard to the car park. Go to page 12.

As chemicals are involved, the fire brigade is called.
"Thank goodness we were warned about this stuff," says the fire chief. "This could have been a tragedy. These are lethal chemicals."

You hear someone in the crowd say, "Those chemicals were going to the factory. That teacher always said they were up to no good. Let's go and see her."
The police sergeant walks over to you.
"We'll need you to make a statement," he says. "Can you come back to the station with me?"

People are drifting down to Jill's.
Go with them. Go to page 24.
Or go to the police station. Go to page 40.

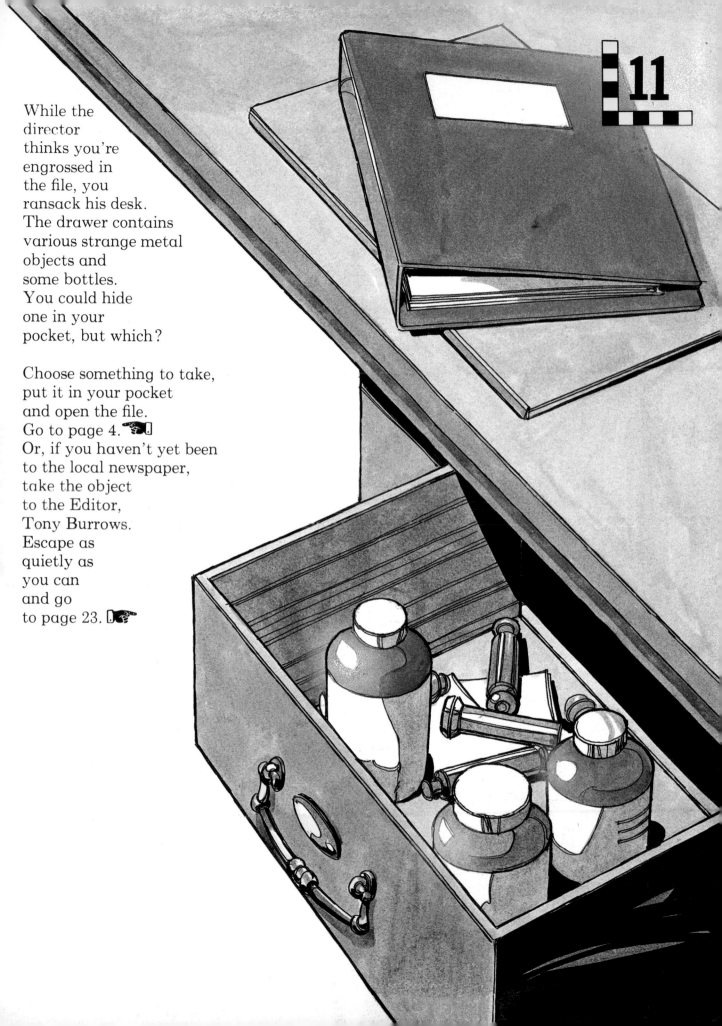

While the director thinks you're engrossed in the file, you ransack his desk. The drawer contains various strange metal objects and some bottles. You could hide one in your pocket, but which?

Choose something to take, put it in your pocket and open the file.
Go to page 4.
Or, if you haven't yet been to the local newspaper, take the object to the Editor, Tony Burrows. Escape as quietly as you can and go to page 23.

12 "Take my word," says the guard. "All we make is perfume. Here, give this box of samples to your mother with our compliments."
You take the box from him, and he goes on, "Please don't come back. I get awfully depressed when we have nosey people about."

He drives you down to the main road, and lets you out.

If you want to cross the marsh to the village, go to page 28.
Or take the main road towards the village. Go to page 5.

The van you saw on the way to the factory has crashed outside the children's playground. A crowd gathers. The police arrive and question the shaken driver. As you approach, you hear him insist, "It's only bleach in the jars."

If you want to tell the sergeant that the driver is lying, go to page 10.
Or, if you don't want to call attention to yourself, keep your ears open and go to page 15.

The helicopter circles at a discreet distance.

The explosion sends a great column of burning gas into the air, and blasts a shallow crater in the soft ground. As the dust settles, you see the helicopter fly away.

As you walk over to the crater, something shiny catches your eye: three silver coins. They look very old.

Could they have been thrown up by the explosion? Are there more down there? You scour the surrounding grass, but find nothing.

Where do you go now?

If you want to go to the factory, go to page 41.

Or, if you want to go to Jill's, go to page 29.

"Get away from there!" the driver orders, waving at the van. A little girl jumps down from the back. You hear her whine, "Don't feel well."

No one takes any notice until the child begins to choke, at first quietly, then violently, her face turning from blotchy red to deathly white. She is horribly sick. You run to the police sergeant.

"Quickly," you beg, "Call an ambulance. That little girl's inhaled dangerous fumes."

"What do you know about it?" asks the sergeant. "Perhaps you'd better come along with me and explain."

Someone runs the child to hospital. You hear her father say, "That factory's to blame. I'm off to Jill Foster's. She warned us about this –"

Go with him to Jill's, on page 24.☞

Or go to the police station on page 40.☞

You realise that you should never have come on foot. A mist is rising and you must find shelter. There are only two places to go.

The factory is nearer. You might manage to avoid the security guard, but it would be risky. Or you could keep going towards the old church. If Jill's friends have any sense, they'll have taken shelter there by now.

If you want to try the factory, go to page 21.

Or, if you want to go to the church, go to page 33.

Four hours later, you and the director land.

Two men meet you. One says to the director, "You have not done well. We shall speak of this later."

The other says to you, "Glad to see you're all right. I'm from the Embassy."

You ask what has happened.

"Police organised a raid on this chap's factory – called it operation Blue Light. Thought that you might be a prisoner – you weren't there, so they put two and two together. Pity he made it here. We can't extradite him. Still, no doubt he'll try again."

So you are safe!

"Only one thing," continues the Embassy man. "You'll have to pay your air fare home. Got two hundred and fifty pounds on you, I hope."

18

You climb into the helicopter to have a look at the package. Behind the seats you find some strange canisters, but before you can examine them, the pilot arrives. Luckily, he doesn't look into the back, but fastens his safety belt and starts the engine.

What do you do now?
The pilot may not be going far. Helicopters are often used for short hops across parts of the marsh too water-logged to bear lorries or cars.

If you want to get into the factory quickly, make your presence known to the pilot. He will take you to the factory and hand you over to a security guard.

Go to page 9.

Or, if you prefer to arrive at the factory under your own steam and secretly, stay hidden and go to page 37.

Without giving away any details, you manage to tell everyone that the police will be taking action against the factory.

Gradually Jill restores order.

The villagers agree to wait for a day or two to see if the police and the pollution inspector close the factory.

"We'd better have a watch dog committee to make sure nothing like this happens again," someone suggests. Everyone agrees.

You aren't invited to take part in the raid, of course, but as you spend so much time watching the factory, you soon find out when it is starting. If you want to see the action, go to page 26. 👉

20

Though Jill drove fast, some of the villagers got there first. They took the security guards by surprise and broke into the laboratory. They have caused a lot of damage. You notice the familiar smell of paint, but it is much stronger than before.

Jill is distraught.
"That smell is VC2," she tells you. "It's leaking – who knows how much has already escaped. This is the worst thing that could happen. A few litres could make the marsh sterile for years: no birds, no wildlife, no grass. It happened in Italy. They had to concrete over whole fields."

You leave Jill to evacuate the factory while you telephone the fire brigade and the police.

You determine to be more careful in the next adventure.

You are caught almost at once. The director is furious.

"All my work is ruined by fools like you," he shouts. "I'm leaving. But don't think I'm leaving you to put the police on my trail. You're coming to my client's country. They have certain schools to teach you good behaviour."

He orders the security guard to take you to the helicopter pad.

On the way, the guard pauses to light a cigarette. Out of the corner of his mouth he whispers, "Do the words 'Blue Light' mean anything to you?"

If they do, go to page 42.

Or, if the words don't mean anything to you, go to the helicopter.

Go to page 17.

Farther on you notice a strong smell, rather like paint, coming from the factory. Suddenly you come across a terrible sight. A starling, wheeling and floundering on the road.

You pick it up, and hurry on.

The smell of paint fades. Gradually the starling becomes quiet. Then, with a huge effort, it breaks free and flies away.

Hurry after the van and go to page 43.
Or change your mind and go on to Jill's. Go to page 38.

The door to the local newspaper office is open, so you walk in, to find Tony Burrows standing among total chaos.

"What happened?" you gasp.

"I've been out all day," he replies. "I've just come back – to this."

"Is anything missing?" you ask.

"Oh yes," he groans. "My notes, the telephoto pictures of the marsh, the samples of dying plants, the analysis we commissioned of the effluent on Long Pond . . . everything – everything to connect the factory with pollution."

You ask Tony if you can help him to clear up.

"No thanks," he says. "You'd be more useful at the hall. The factory director has organised a public meeting. I'd like to know what happens."

If you want to help Tony, go to the meeting. Go to page 32.

Or, if you want to go home first, walk through the village to page 13.

24

A sort of protest meeting is going on outside Jill's front door. More and more people gather. They sound angry.

"Perfume my foot: dangerous chemicals!"

"What can we do?"

"Let's go down there and sort them out."

Jill objects, "No, that's not the way. Someone might be hurt."

No one listens. This is going to lead to an ugly incident. Can you stop it? Do you know the meaning of the code-words 'Blue Light'?

If you do, go to page 19.
Or, if you don't know what the words mean, you and Jill will have to follow the enraged villagers to the factory. Go to page 20.

"Right," says Tony, "I'll get a few photographs of the marsh. But for the real story, we need to know what the factory is making, and if it's harmful."

"It's a pity we can't get really close to the factory," says Jill, "but they'll never let me up there."

She asks if you would like to go to the meeting and tell everybody what you saw on the marsh.

You know you could get a close look at the factory because you know the farm house so well.

If you want to go to the meeting, stay at Jill's and go to page 46. ☛
Or go off to the factory for a closer look. Go to page 41. ☛

26

"Operation Blue Light!" says the security guard.

Someone comes up to you, leading an excited alsation dog. You recognise the local police sergeant.

"I reckon we've won this round," he says. "That's the end of this firm."

"I take it you've arrested the director?" asks the security guard.

"Oh yes. He tried to get away in the 'copter, but he had engine trouble."

"He would," says the security guard, dangling a bunch of coloured wires. "I borrowed these."

"That's it then," says the sergeant. "Mind, there must be a dozen factories that we don't know about, just as dangerous as this one."

"Still," replies the security guard. "Mustn't be greedy. One at a time."

By the time Jill has recovered, her friends from the museum arrive, and she is soon feeling better.

"I'm going to hold the meeting I've planned," she says. "I'm trying to start an action group to fight the pollution from the factory, and we're meeting in the village hall."

Jill's friends decide to set up camp, and ask her to join them later.

You're not sure that there is enough evidence to convince the villagers of the danger of the factory.

If you want to go to Jill's meeting, go to page 3.

Or, if you want to investigate the factory, go to page 41.

28 Coming this way was a mistake. A storm is brewing. You must find shelter.
It's risky but you could hide somewhere in the factory – perhaps the cellar?
Even if you are caught, what harm could come to you?
The old church is farther away, but much safer.

If you want to try your luck at the factory, go to page 21.

Or, if you want to go to the church, go to page 45.

You tell Jill the story of the explosion and she says, "You were lucky not to be hurt!"
After looking at the coins, she telephones a friend at the local museum.
"Can you draw a map of exactly where you found the coins?" she asks. "My friend is extremely interested. She's going to bring one or two other archaeologists over. They'll camp by the church and sink a few test trenches."

You wonder what to do next.
"I bet Tony Burrows would like to see the coins," says Jill. "He was very interested in the samples of polluted grasses you gave him. We might persuade him to print an article on the marsh past and present."

If you agree with Jill, take the coins to the local newspaper office on page 23. 👈
Or offer to show her the crater first and go via the marsh. Go to page 44. 👉

30 Last night's storm has eroded the beach and uncovered the remains of an ancient shipwreck.

"Beautiful," says one of the archaeologists. "A Viking longship." "We'll have to work fast," says another, "to get her out and away before the tourist season." "We don't have many tourists here," you begin. "You do now," interrupts an archaeologist. "They'll be flocking here."

That should put an end to the factory's activities – they won't be very keen on sightseers! All you have to do now is wait.

The place looks deserted. You examine the bits of machinery. They remind you of the aircraft engines you've seen in museums.

Then you notice the plans on the table. You take one from underneath the pile and slip it into your pocket.

If you want to look in the factory's laboratory, go to page 34.
Or go to the director's office and, pretending to be doing a school project, ask if you can interview him. Go to page 36.

You arrive in time to hear the director address the villagers.

"We are a very simple, very small factory. We make perfume. We always try to smell sweet."

The audience laughs.

"Now, I invite you all. Very soon we're having an Open Day. Come and see our factory. Look at everything. Bring the kids. You'll enjoy it."

There is clapping and people are saying, "That's a good idea. Fair enough."

You realise everybody has been taken in, and leave in disgust.

Walk away from the village across the marsh. Go to page 28.

Or into the village along the main street. Go to page 13.

You meet Jill's friends.
"We've got a radio," says one. "We'll let the police know you're safe and they can pass the news on to your family." After a sleepless night in the musty, leaky church, listening to the storm raging outside, you breakfast with the archaeologists. One takes you aside.
"Jill told me about the factory," she says. "The others don't know, but I'm keeping an eye on it."

She invites you to visit the dig.
If you would like to go, go to page 30.
Or, if you think that you ought to start for home, go to page 13.

As you close the door behind you, you run into a security guard. "How long have you been here?" he demands. "And what have you been doing? Turn out your pockets."

If you have taken something from the factory, the guard will take you to the director. Go to page 36.

Or, if you don't have anything belonging to the factory, he will take you to page 9.

On the way, the van driver stops by a landing pad at the side of the road. He takes a small package and carries it across to a waiting helicopter, leaving it on the passenger seat.

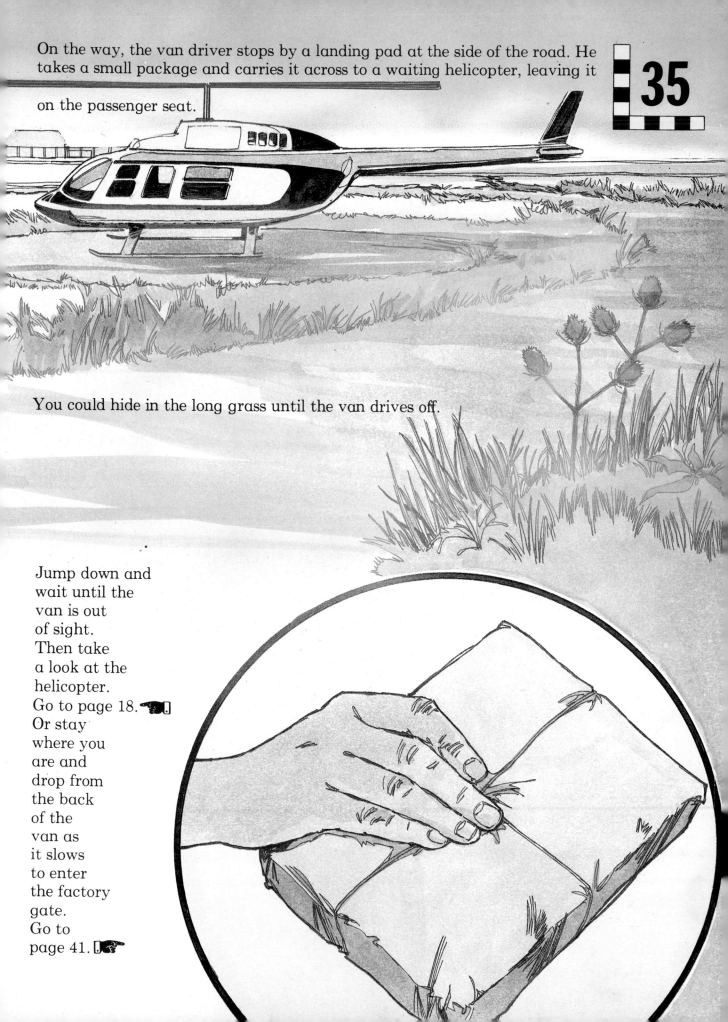

You could hide in the long grass until the van drives off.

Jump down and wait until the van is out of sight. Then take a look at the helicopter. Go to page 18. Go to page 18. Or stay where you are and drop from the back of the van as it slows to enter the factory gate. Go to page 41.

The director doesn't seem surprised to see you.

"Let me offer you a drink," he begins. "We're always pleased to have guests, though usually we invite them." He pushes a bulging file across the desk, saying, "Please read this. It'll interest you, I think." Then he walks out of the room.

How much time do you have?

If you think you have long enough, search through his desk and go to page 11.

Or, if you think that the director will be back in a moment, open the file and go to page 4.

The flight takes only two minutes. Then you land by the old church, deserted since it began to subside.

The pilot takes the package from the passenger seat and puts it on the ground. Then he piles the canisters around it and, attaching a wire to the package, begins to walk backwards, unrolling the wire as he goes.

Suddenly you realise: he's going to blow the canisters up! Wriggle through the long grass and, while the pilot's back is turned, leap over the churchyard wall. Then you can watch him from page 14.
Or get away fast and make your way to Jill's on page 38.

38

Jill is being interviewed by Tony Burrows, Editor of the local newspaper.

"I'm starting an action group. In fact, we're meeting in the village hall in half an hour," Jill tells him.

You realise they are discussing the factory.

"Ever since it opened," says Jill, "there's been twice as much traffic. Helicopters, vans, motorbikes."

"All right, there are problems," says Tony. "But what evidence is there of real pollution?"

If you think you should tell Tony what you saw on the way over, go to page 25.

Or wait to see what Jill has discovered. Go to page 6.

You find the newspaper in the library and search for the article. You learn that a factory near Turin, Italy, has been closed following the discovery that it was producing an illegal fuel additive. VC2 produces noxious fumes which have a characteristic odour, described as 'like strong paint' and which cause severe nausea.
Unless stored in airtight lead canisters, VC2 evaporates within twelve hours.

If you want to go to the local newspaper office and persuade Tony Burrows to print your story of the threat posed by the factory, go to page 23.

Or, if you want evidence, go back to the marsh and try to enter the factory. Go to page 41.

"Thank you for co-operating," says the sergeant. "This gentleman is an inspector. Not a police inspector, an environmental pollution inspector. Please tell him all you know about the factory."

You do.

"Right," says the inspector. "We've been watching that place. Now we can get a warrant and raid it."

"You've been a great help," the sergeant tells you. "Don't talk to anyone about this, will you?"

He turns to the inspector, saying, "Let's get on, shall we? Operation Blue Light!"

You leave the station. If you want to go to Jill's, go to page 24.

Or, if you want to go back to the factory for another look, go to page 21.

It all looks very different from when it was a
farm, but you still know your way around.
You find your way through the disused boiler
house at the back. It leads to the corridor between
two large downstairs rooms. There are two doors.
One must be the laboratory, the other an office.

If you choose the door on the left, go to page 8.

Or, if you choose the door on the right, go to page 7.

41

You tell the security guard what the words mean to you and he says, "Right! Quickly, get in here!"

He thrusts you into a shed full of bits of equipment and tools, obviously used for repairing the helicopters.

"Stay quiet," he hisses. "I'll be back in a minute." You crouch behind a stripped engine until the guard returns. He joins you, whispering, "Not long now. I've wrapped up a dummy in blankets and put it in the 'copter. Told the director I had to sedate you!"

Suddenly the courtyard is full of running figures. The security guard dashes from the shed, hurrying back to the factory.

If you want to escape while you can, go home, forget the factory and avoid the marsh in future. Or, if you want to investigate, follow the guard and demand to know what's going on. Go to page 26.

You see the van making its way to the factory. The driver is concentrating on the difficult bend. He probably wouldn't notice if you scrambled onto the back of his van.

If you want to steal a ride, go to page 35.
Or keep walking. Make for the higher ground overlooking the factory. Go to page 2.

You lead the way through the marsh carefully keeping to the safe ground. But you go too quickly for Jill. Hearing her call out, you turn, and see her sinking!

You cannot go for help. She could drown before you get back. You must rescue her yourself.

You lie as flat as you can on the ground in front of her, and dig your feet in. Then you lock your arms under her shoulders. Slowly, you wriggle backwards, pulling her as you go.

Finally, she scrambles free.

You have no choices for once. You must take Jill home right away. Go to page 27.

You are not the only person to take shelter in the church. The pews seem to be full of archaeologists! "Don't worry," says one. "We'll call the police on our radio. So your family will know you're safe."
The storm goes on until first light, hail lashing the windows and high winds shaking the church to its foundations.
You breakfast with the archaeologists and they invite you to visit their dig.

If you think that it would be better to make for home, go to page 13. ☞
Or, if you would like to see an archaeological dig, go to page 30. ☞

Jill asks the villagers, "Which are the worst problems caused by the factory?" "Traffic," answers someone in the back row. "Noise," says someone from the front.

"– and jobs. Why don't they employ any local people?"

You try to explain about the pollution problem.
"Oh, that's a lot of nonsense," interrupts someone. "A little dirt never hurt anybody."

No one wants to listen to you.

If you want to try to get some evidence to convince the villagers about the pollution, go to the factory on page 41.
Or, if you have already got some evidence of pollution, or you think that the local newspaper may have found some, go to see Tony Burrows in his office on page 23.